Hamsters DON'T Fight Fires!

By Andrew Root   Illustrated by Jessica Olien

HARPER

An Imprint of HarperCollins Publishers

Hamsters Don't Fight Fires!

Text copyright © 2017 by Andrew Root

Illustrations copyright © 2017 by Jessica Olien

All rights reserved. Manufactured in China.

Library of Congress Control Number: 2016952344

ISBN 978-0-06-245294-8

The artist used Photoshop to create the digital illustrations for this book.

Typography by Rachel Zegar

17 18 19 20 21 SCP 10 9 8 7 6 5 4 3 2 1

❖

First Edition

For North & Isa
—A.R.

To the people in room 514
—J.O.

Hugo was a hamster.

Hugo was many things.
He was:

helpful,

polite,

generous,

a great cook,

a fast runner,

a slow eater,

and a fantastic dancer.

However, Hugo was not:

strong,

tall,

able to sing,

or particularly good at bowling.

And Hugo was certainly not a firefighter.

Still, Hugo had always wanted to
be a firefighter.

Ever since he was young, he loved
the flashing lights of the fire engines
and the awesome suits that the
firefighters wore.

Hugo also loved helping others,
which is exactly what firefighters
get to do all day long.

After all, who needs more help than a scaredy-cat stuck in a tree?

Hamster, can you help?

Or a chef who can't cook for his guests because his barbecue is on the fritz?

"You should become a firefighter, Hugo! You'd be great at it," Hugo's friend Scarlett said to him one day.

"I'm sure it would be difficult, but you should never be afraid to try something new," Scarlett explained.

"Look at me. I may be a snake, but someday I'll be the first reptile astronaut to blast into outer space."

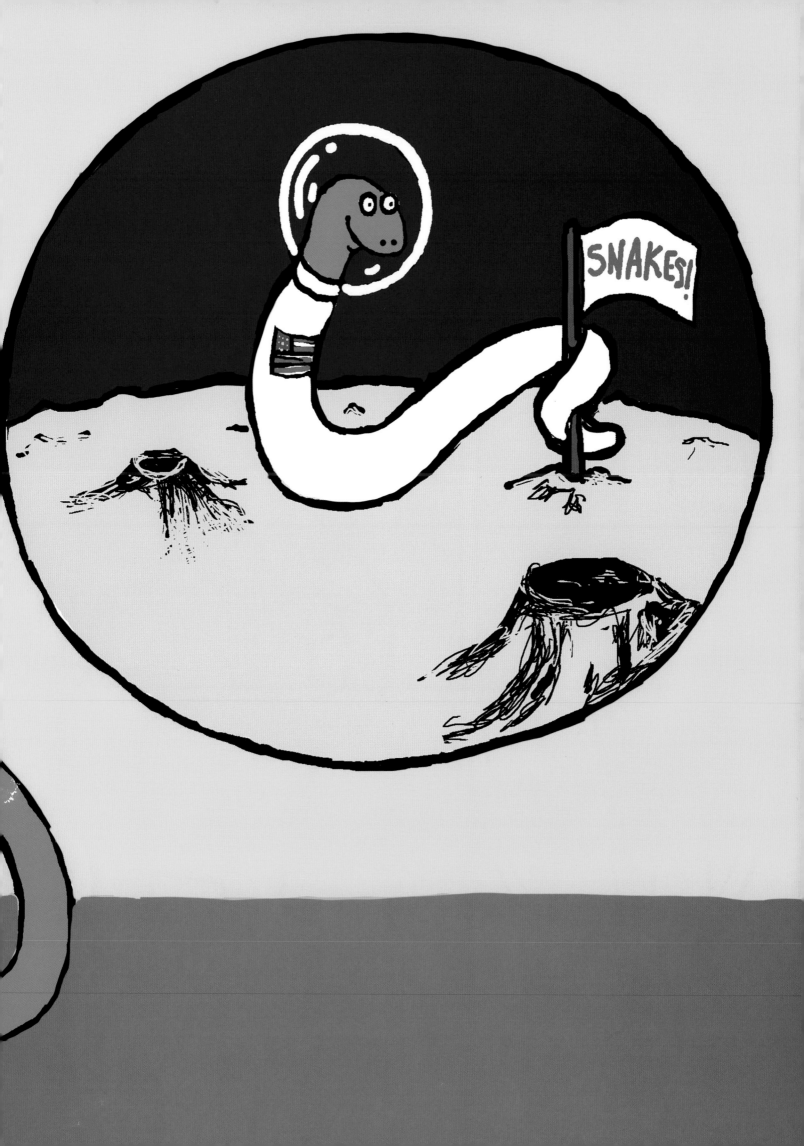

Hugo was still nervous, but he decided that Scarlett was right. Even though he was small, perhaps he should try to become a firefighter.

He gathered his courage, walked down to the station house, and convinced the fire chief to give him a chance.

However, things did not look good when:

He put on a fire suit
that was much too big,

sprayed the fire hose
that was much too heavy,

attempted to drive the fire engine
that was much too fast,

and tried to slide down the fire
pole that was much too high.

"I am much too small," he said. "How can I help when I am not big enough to slide, drive, or spray the hose like the other firefighters?"

Hugo was ready to give up and go home.

Hugo tried to stay out of the way of the others, but
in all the rush and confusion, he was given a fire suit
that was much too big . . .

. . . and somehow ended up on the back of the truck.

When they arrived at the Great Woods, the firefighters rushed into action, unraveling hoses, setting up the ladders, and spraying water all around.

Hugo watched the action and wished
he was big enough to help. Then he
looked up and saw a baby bird trapped
in a nest at the tippy top of a tree.
He told the firefighters about the
bird, but no one knew what to do.

The tree was so tall that none of
the ladders could reach the nest.
   The branches were too old and
too weak for any of the bigger
firefighters to make such a
dangerous climb.

CHEEP!
CHEEP!

As the flames grew higher, Hugo knew what he had to do. He might not be a real firefighter, but the little bird needed his help.

Gathering all his courage and strength, Hugo ran to the tree and started to climb.

Hugo was very quick and soon he reached the nest.

With the scared baby bird carefully balanced on his back, Hugo rushed down the tree to safety.

Back on the ground, all the firefighters were cheering for Hugo!

He had done what no one else could.

The baby bird was safe and back in her mother's wings.

Hugo's bravery had saved the day!

The fire chief came over and exclaimed, "I had my doubts, Hugo. But today you showed everyone that there is more to being a firefighter than how big you are. We would be proud to have you as part of the team!"

All the firefighters clapped for Hugo and lifted
him up on their shoulders in congratulations. The
local newspaper even took a picture. It was on the
front page the very next day.

Hugo became the newest member of the North
Creek Fire Station.
And, as it turned out, he also:

could make an amazing
four-alarm firehouse chili,

excelled at teaching the younger
animals about fire safety,

knew all the shortcuts for navigating the
fire engine around town,

could climb the tallest ladder to
rescue the scarediest cat,

and was small enough to fix even the
most difficult broken barbecue.

Who would've guessed that you could even order
a special hamster-size fire suit from the internet!

Endlessstuff.com

REAL
FIRE SUIT

Size:
Mouse-rat

1

Customers also bought:

Lizard tutu | Party hats | Lightbulbs

Hugo was a hamster.
He was still:

helpful,

polite,

generous, a great cook,

a fast runner,

a slow eater,

and a fantastic dancer.

But now he was also a firefighter!
And he could not have been any happier.